Playing
F
Alexandre Dumas'

The Three Musketeers
FOR KIDS
(The melodramatic version!)

For 7-17+ actors, or kids of all ages who want to have fun!
Creatively modified by
Brendan P. Kelso
Cover illustrations by Shana Hallmeyer and Adam Watson
Cover Characters by Ron Leishman
Special Contributor: Asif Zamir

3 Melodramatic Modifications of Shakespeare's Play
for 3 different group sizes:

7-12+ actors

11-14 actors

12-17+ actors

Table Of Contents

Foreword	Pg 4
School, Afterschool, and Summer classes	Pg 6
Performance Rights	Pg 6
7-12+ Actors	Pg 8
11-14+ Actors	Pg 30
12-17+ Actors	Pg 54
Pronunciation Key	Pg 78
Special Thanks	Pg 79
Sneak Peeks at other Playing With Plays	Pg 80
About the Author	Pg 102

To my wife,
for never being afraid to go on an adventure!
Carpe Diem!

-BPK

Playing with Plays™ - Alexandre Dumas' The Three Musketeers for Kids

Copyright © 2004-2020 by Brendan P. Kelso, Playing with Plays LLC
Some characters on the cover are ©Ron Leishman ToonClipart.com

All rights reserved. No part of this book may be reproduced in any form or by any electronic or mechanical means, including photocopying, recording, information storage or retrieval systems now known or to be invented, without permission in writing from the publisher, except by a reviewer, who may quote brief passages in a review, written for inclusion within a periodical. Any members of education institutions wishing to photocopy part or all of the work for classroom use, or publishers who would like to obtain permission to include the work in an anthology, should send their inquiries to the publisher. We monitor the internet for cases of piracy and copyright infringement/violations. We will pursue all cases within the full extent of the law.

Whenever a Playing With Plays play is produced, the following must be included on all programs, printing and advertising for the play: © Brendan P. Kelso, Playing with Plays LLC, www.PlayingWithPlays.com. All rights reserved.

CAUTION: Professionals and amateurs are hereby warned that these plays are subject to a royalty. They are fully protected, in whole, in part, or in any form under the copyright laws of the United States, Canada, the British Empire, and all other countries of the Copyright Union, and are subject to royalty. All rights, including professional, amateur, motion picture, radio, television, recitation, public reading, internet, and any method of photographic reproduction are strictly reserved.

For performance rights please see page 6 of this book or contact:

contact@PlayingWithPlays.com

-Please note, for certain circumstances, we do waive copyright and performance fees.
Rules subject to change

www.PlayingWithPlays.com

Printed in the United States of America
Published by Playing With Plays

ISBN-13: 978-1542718462
ISBN-10: 1542718465

Foreword

When I was in high school there was something about Shakespeare that appealed to me. Not that I understood it mind you, but there were clear scenes and images that always stood out in my mind. Romeo & Juliet, "Romeo, Romeo; wherefore art thou Romeo?"; Julius Caesar, "Et tu Brute"; Macbeth, "Double, Double, toil and trouble"; Hamlet, "to be or not to be"; A Midsummer Night's Dream, all I remember about this was a wickedly cool fairy and something about a guy turning into a donkey that I thought was pretty funny. It was not until I started analyzing Shakespeare's plays as an actor that I realized one very important thing, I still didn't understand them. Seriously though, it's tough enough for adults, let alone kids. Then it hit me, why don't I make a version that kids could perform, but make it easy for them to understand with a splash of Shakespeare lingo mixed in? And voila! A melodramatic masterpiece was created! They are intended to be melodramatically fun!

THE PLAYS: There are 3 plays within this book, for three different group sizes. The reason: to allow educators or parents to get the story across to their children regardless of the size of their group. As you read through the plays, there are several lines that are highlighted. These are actual lines from the original book. I am a little more particular about the kids saying these lines verbatim. But the rest, well... have fun!

The entire purpose of this book is to instill the love of a classic story, as well as drama, into the kids.

And when you have children who have a passion for something, they will start to teach themselves, with or without school.

These plays are intended for pure fun. Please DO NOT have the kids learn these lines verbatim, that would be a complete waste of creativity. But do have them basically know their lines and improvise wherever they want as long as it pertains to telling the story. Because that is the goal of an actor: to tell the story. In A Midsummer Night's Dream, I once had a student playing Quince question me about one of her lines, "but in the actual story, didn't the Mechanicals state that 'they would hang us'?" I thought for a second and realized that she had read the story with her mom, and she was right. So I let her add the line she wanted and it added that much more fun, it made the play theirs. I have had kids throw water on the audience, run around the audience, sit in the audience, lose their pumpkin pants (size 30 around a size 15 doesn't work very well, but makes for some great humor!) and most importantly, die all over the stage. The kids love it.

One last note: if you want some educational resources, loved our plays, want to tell the world how much your kids loved performing Shakespeare, want to insult someone with our Shakespeare Insult Generator, or are just a fan of Shakespeare, then hop on our website and have fun:

PlayingWithPlays.com

With these notes, I'll see you on the stage, have fun, and break a leg!

SCHOOL, AFTERSCHOOL, and SUMMER classes

I've been teaching these plays as afterschool and summer programs for quite some time. Many people have asked what the program is, therefore, I have put together a basic formula so any teacher or parent can follow and have melodramatic success! As well, many teachers use my books in a variety of ways. You can view the formula and many more resources on my website at: PlayingWithPlays.com

- Brendan

OTHER PLAYS AND FULL LENGTH SCRIPTS

We have over 25 different titles, as well as a full-length play in 4-acts for theatre groups: Shakespeare's Hilarious Tragedies. You can see all of our other titles on our website here: PlayingWithPlays.com/books

As well, you can see a sneak peek at some of those titles at the back of this book.

And, if you ever have any questions, please don't hesitate to ask at: Contact@PlayingWithPlays.com

ROYALTIES

If you have any questions about royalties or performance licenses, here are the basic guidelines:

1) Please contact us! We always LOVE to hear about a school or group performing our books! We would also love to share photos and brag about your program as well! (with your permission, of course)

2) If you are a group and DO NOT charge your kids to be in this production, contact us about discounted copyright fees (one way or another, we will make this work for you!) You are NOT required to buy a book per kid (but, we will still send you some really cool Shakespeare tattoos for your kids!)

3) If you are a group and DO charge your kids to be in the production, (i.e. afterschool program, summer camp) we ask that you purchase a book per kid. Contact us as we will give you a bulk discount (10 books or more) and send some really cool press on Shakespeare tattoos!

4) If you are a group and DO NOT charge the audience to see the plays, please see our website FAQs to see if you are eligible to waive the performance royalties (most performances are eligible).

5) If you are a group and DO charge the audience to see the performance, please see our website FAQs for performance licensing fees (this includes performances for donations and competitions).

Any other questions or comments, please see our website or email us at:

contact@PlayingWithPlays.com

The 15-Minute or so The Three Musketeers

By Alexandre Dumas'
Creatively modified by
Brendan P. Kelso

7-12+ Actors

CAST OF CHARACTERS:

D'ARTAGNAN: Young, arrogant, wannabe musketeer; awesome swordsman

ATHOS: Musketeer #1 – quiet and strong

ARAMIS: Musketeer #2 – quiet and passive

PORTHOS: Musketeer #3 – loud and hungry

[3]**CARDINAL RICHELIEU:** Our villain and evil mastermind

[1]**MILADY de WINTER:** Wicked and cunning thief and assassin

[4]**KING LOUIS XIII:** King of France and not too smart

[1]**QUEEN ANNE:** Queen of France, smarter

[2]**GEORGE VILLIERS, THE DUKE OF BUCKINGHAM:** England; he likes the queen

CONSTANCE: D'Artagnan's girlfriend – super cute

[3]**COUNT de ROCHEFORT:** Cardinal's evil right-hand man

[3]**JUSSAC:** Cardinal's guard and best swordsman in France, until D'Artagnan comes along

The same actors can play the following parts:
[1]Queen and Milady
[2]Duke and any Musketeer
[3]Cardinal, Rochefort, and Jussac
[4]King and any Musketeer

There are also random guards that die during the play

There's a simple pronunciation key for the names and many words throughout the play, located at the back of the book.

ACT 1 SCENE 1

(enter D'ARTAGNAN)

D'ARTAGNAN: *(to audience)* Well, I'm going to travel to Paris to become a Musketeer! I know what you're thinking...that's a great idea! I mean, so what if I'm not even 20 yet, I doubt I'll get in ANY trouble, and hey, I might even find a girl that likes me! Ha, hah, adventure awaits!

(exits)

ACT 1 SCENE 2

(enter D'ARTAGNAN riding a fake horse; enter ROCHEFORT)

ROCHEFORT: *(to audience)* That is one ugly horse!

D'ARTAGNAN: Sir, tell me what you are laughing at.

ROCHEFORT: Oh. Your horse...very ugly.

D'ARTAGNAN: Don't insult my horse! Let's fight!

ROCHEFORT: Why, my good fellow, you must be mad! *(points behind D'ARTAGNAN)* Oh look, an elephant!

D'ARTAGNAN: Where? *(ROCHEFORT hits D'ARTAGNAN on the head, he falls to the ground)*

D'ARTAGNAN: Man, that wasn't fair! Who are you?

ROCHEFORT: Ha, hah! Just call me the man of Meung. Goodbye!

(ROCHEFORT exits laughing evilly; D'ARTAGNAN exits holding his head)

ACT 1 SCENE 3

(enter 3 MUSKETEERS who stand downstage: ATHOS center; PORTHOS left; ARAMIS right)

ATHOS: *(to audience)* We are the Three Musketeers. I am Athos.

PORTHOS: *(striking a gallant pose)* I am Porthos.

ARAMIS: *(sitting down to read a book)* And I am Aramis.

(enter D'ARTAGNAN)

D'ARTAGNAN: I must catch that man of Meung! *(bumps into ATHOS)* Excuse me, but I am in a hurry.

ATHOS: You are in a hurry?

D'ARTAGNAN: Duh! I'm running across the stage; you are in my way. I did not do it intentionally and I said 'Excuse me.' So, move it buddy, before you get hurt!

ATHOS: Monsieur, you are not polite.

D'ARTAGNAN: I warn you, If I wasn't running after someone... I would....

ATHOS: You would what? Monsieur Man-in-a-hurry, you can find me without running – ME....for a duel. Let's meet at the Carmes-Deschaux. About noon.

D'ARTAGNAN: Where? *(pause)* Whatever! I will be there! Now, out of my way! *(shoves away ATHOS, and runs around stage; ATHOS exits; D'ARTAGNAN runs into PORTHOS and falls to the ground, while PORTHOS doesn't move)*

PORTHOS: Bless me! What do you think you're doing?

D'ARTAGNAN: Excuse me, I was running after someone. *(realizing how big PORTHOS is)* Whoa! You're one big ugly dude....uhhhh, I mean, monsieur.

PORTHOS: What?! Insult me? At one o'clock then, let's duel.

D'ARTAGNAN: Very well, at one o'clock, then. See ya! *(D'ARTAGNAN runs around stage again, PORTHOS exits; ARAMIS gets up, walks across stage and drops handkerchief accidentally from pocket)*

D'ARTAGNAN: Sir! You dropped your handkerchief! *(picks it up)*

ARAMIS: I did not drop it, and it is not mine!

D'ARTAGNAN: What? You have lied twice, monsieur, for I saw it fall from your hands.

ARAMIS: Did you just call me a liar? Well, I will teach you how to behave yourself. Two o'clock. Duel.

D'ARTAGNAN: Really? Sure, why not. Oh, and take your handkerchief, you're going to need it!

(they bow to each other; ARAMIS exits)

D'ARTAGNAN: *(to audience)* Aghhhhhhh!!! Seriously? Three Musketeers in the next three hours!!! But at least, if I am killed, I shall be killed by a Musketeer!

(D'ARTAGNAN exits)

ACT 1 SCENE 4

(ATHOS and D'ARTAGNAN enter)

ATHOS: Glad you could make it. I have engaged two of my friends as seconds.

D'ARTAGNAN: Seconds?

ATHOS: Yeah, they make sure we fight fair. Oh, here they are now!

(enter ARAMIS and PORTHOS singing, "Bad boys, bad boys, whatcha gonna do...")

PORTHOS: Hey! I'm fighting him in an hour. I am going to fight... because...well... I am going to fight!

ARAMIS: And I fight him at two o'clock! Ours is a theological quarrel. *(does a thinking pose)*

D'ARTAGNAN: Yeah, yeah, yeah.... I'll get to you soon!

ATHOS: We are the Three Musketeers; Athos, Porthos, and Aramis.

D'ARTAGNAN: Whatever, Ethos, Pathos, and Logos, let's just finish this! *(swords crossed and are about to fight; enter JUSSAC and cardinal's guards)*

PORTHOS: The cardinal's guards! Sheathe your swords, gentlemen.

JUSSAC: Dueling is illegal! You are under arrest!

ARAMIS: *(to ATHOS and PORTHOS)* There's three of us, let's get him!

D'ARTAGNAN: *(steps forward to join them)* It appears to me we are four! I have the spirit; my heart is that of a Musketeer.

PORTHOS: Great! I love fighting! Go get him, kid!

(D'ARTAGNAN says "Fight, fight fight!...Fight, fight, fight!" as he fights JUSSAC and it's a big fight; JUSSAC is wounded and exits; the 3 MUSKETEERS cheer)

ATHOS: Well done!

ARAMIS: And we don't have to kill you now!

PORTHOS: And let's get some food, too! I'm hungry!

D'ARTAGNAN: *(to audience)* This is fun!

(ALL exit)

ACT 2 SCENE 1

(enter D'ARTAGNAN carrying a message)

D'ARTAGNAN: *(reading letter)* A beautiful maiden has been kidnapped by the cardinal. Her name is Constance and she works for the queen. She was taken by a man with a scar on his face! *(rips letter)* Why, that's my man of Meung! *(yelling out)* I will help find you!

CONSTANCE: *(from off stage)* Thank you!

D'ARTAGNAN: *(yelling out)* Hey Musketeers!

(enter ATHOS, ARAMIS, PORTHOS)

ARAMIS: Hello.

ATHOS: Hello!

PORTHOS: Hello!!!

D'ARTAGNAN: Hello... beautiful girl, vengeance, adventure, going against the cardinal... and possibly even death... you in?

ATHOS: He just said we might die!

PORTHOS: He sure did!

ARAMIS: And we sure might!

3 MUSKETEERS: We're in!

(ALL exit)

ACT 2 SCENE 2

(enter D'ARTAGNAN and CONSTANCE)

D'ARTAGNAN: *(to audience)* There is Constance and wow! I mean like, a whole lot of WOW!

CONSTANCE: Excuse me?

D'ARTAGNAN: Uhhhh… nothing… I mean, you have the sweetest smile in the world!

CONSTANCE: Thanks. *(pause)* Who are you?

D'ARTAGNAN: Oh! I'm D'Artagnan. Your dad asked me to find you, and well, here you are!

CONSTANCE: Right. I just escaped from the cardinal's guards. Now, I must go, because I have some super important stuff to do for the queen!

D'ARTAGNAN: You know what? I like you. No… I LOVE you….

CONSTANCE: Aw, how cute… you're funny. I think I love you too!

(ALL exit)

ACT 2 SCENE 3

(CONSTANCE on stage asleep; DUKE knocks)

CONSTANCE: Who is up at this hour? Can't a girl get her beauty rest?!

(enter DUKE)

DUKE: I am the Duke of Buckingham, and I'm here to see the queen.

CONSTANCE: Buttingham?

DUKE: BUCKINGHAM!!!

CONSTANCE: *(yawning)* Oh... you do realize it is two in the morning.

DUKE: Yes, but knowing our countries hate each other, it's probably best to travel in darkness.

CONSTANCE: Whatever. *(yelling offstage)* Oh, Queen!!!

(enter QUEEN)

DUKE: *(to the QUEEN)* I know you're the Queen of France and I'm from England, but I really, really like you!

QUEEN: Easy there, you're cute and all, but I'm married to the king!

DUKE: Speak on, Queen, the sweetness of your voice is AMAZING! I'm not leaving until you accept my never-ending love for you!

QUEEN: Tell ya what, I'll give you my really beautiful necklace the king gave me IF we never see each other again.

DUKE: Uhhhh, okay.

QUEEN: *(to audience)* I sure hope this doesn't get me in trouble later!

DUKE: *(QUEEN hands necklace to DUKE)* Nice knowing you... but, if you need anything you have my number!

QUEEN: Yeah, yeah...

(ALL exit)

ACT 2 SCENE 4

(enter CARDINAL)

CARDINAL: *(to audience)* Well, well! Our spy informed me she saw the queen with the Duke last night! I will use this information and turn the king against the queen. Then, I will take power and rule France! Muahahahahah!!! Now, a special mission. *(calling off stage)* Oh, Milady!!!

(MILADY enters)

MILADY: You called, your eminence?

CARDINAL: Yes. You are a wickedly awesome assassin and thief, and I need you to put those skills to work. Are you up to doing a sinister task?

MILADY: Am I up to it? I am Milady de Winter, the most evil person in this story! You betcha I'm up for it!

CARDINAL: *(to audience)* Wow, she is evil! *(to MILADY)* Please visit the Duke and cut off two diamonds from the queen's necklace.

MILADY: Sounds like fun!

CARDINAL: Awesome, let's laugh evilly while we exit!

MILADY: Yes, let's!

(ALL exit, laughing evilly of course!)

ACT 2 SCENE 5

(enter KING)

KING: Hello Cardinal, what are you laughing about?

CARDINAL: Oh, nothing. How are you?

KING: Couldn't be better!

CARDINAL: Oh... well... that's good.

KING: Why do you say that?

CARDINAL: Well...no...it's not my place.

KING: What? I must know!

CARDINAL: Well sire, it seems that Buckingham has been in Paris five days.

KING: Buckingham in Paris!!! MORDIEU! But, we are enemies! What was he doing here?

CARDINAL: Yeah, about that, rumor has it...no, no... it's too much, sire.

KING: I am the king! You must tell me.

CARDINAL: Your Highness, it seems that he spoke with the queen last night.

KING: No, PARDIEU, no! My wife? But why?

CARDINAL: Well, the Duke IS handsome and powerful, but that can't have ANYTHING to do with it, right?

KING: You think that she deceives me?!

CARDINAL: What?! Nooooo... well...maybe? *(winking to audience)*

KING: What should I do?

CARDINAL: Not sure. *(pause)* Oh, I know, maybe you should show her how faithful you are and throw a big party for her!

KING: How fun!

CARDINAL: Oh, and you can ask her to wear those beautiful diamonds which you gave her, as a token of her love.

KING: Yes, yes, this is good. I'm glad I thought of this! I will tell her right now! *(to audience)* I love it when I come up with great ideas! *(KING exits)*

CARDINAL: *(to audience)* Wow, he's a doofus... taking over power and ruling France will be MUCH easier than I thought! Muahahahah!!!!!

(CARDINAL exits)

ACT 2 SCENE 6

(enter KING, QUEEN, and CONSTANCE)

KING: To show my undying love. I'm throwing a party next week, just for YOU!

QUEEN: That's fantastic! I'm so happy!

KING: And above all, can you wear that beautiful necklace I gave you?

QUEEN: *(to audience)* Uh, oh!

KING: What?

QUEEN: Uhhh, I said, I can't wait to go! So excited!

KING: Great! See ya later! *(KING exits)*

QUEEN: Oh, no! I am lost! I am lost! I just gave that necklace to the Duke!

CONSTANCE: Wait! I have an idea! I'll have my new love, D'Artagnan, and his friends, get your necklace back.

QUEEN: Awesome! I'm so happy again!

(ALL exit)

ACT 3 SCENE 1

(enter D'ARTAGNAN, CONSTANCE, and 3 MUSKETEERS)

CONSTANCE: D'Artagnan, I need you to go to England, get the queen's necklace back from the Duke, and return it within the next two scenes, or the queen will DIE!

ARAMIS: Wow, no pressure.

PORTHOS: This will be fun!

D'ARTAGNAN: So, are you guys in?

ATHOS: One for all, and all for one – That is our motto, is it not?

D'ARTAGNAN: Yes!

(they put their swords together)

ALL: One for all, and all for one!

(ALL exit running off stage)

ACT 3 SCENE 2

(enter D'ARTAGNAN and 3 MUSKETEERS)

PORTHOS: Well men, this journey should be pretty easy!

(enter cardinal's guards)

ARAMIS: Uhhhh, what did you just say?

PORTHOS: Well, it may be a bit harder than I thought! Go on without me, I'll fight them off! FOR FRANCE!!! *(Says, "fight, fight, fight..."; PORTHOS starts fighting them; PORTHOS chases them off stage)*

(D'ARTAGNAN, ARAMIS, and ATHOS run around stage)

ARAMIS: Well, we are getting close.

(CARDINAL'S GUARDS sneak up behind D'ARTAGNAN, ARAMIS, and ATHOS. They start attacking; fight breaks out; everyone saying, "fight, fight, fight..."; GUARDS are killed; ARAMIS is hurt)

ATHOS: Aramis, you're hurt!

ARAMIS: It's just a flesh wound! But, I can proceed no farther! I'll hold off any others!

(ARAMIS exits; ATHOS and D'ARTAGNAN run around stage; GUARDS sneak up behind ATHOS and capture him)

D'ARTAGNAN: Athos!

ATHOS: Go on D'Artagnan! Besides, there's only three of them, I've got this! *(GUARDS take ATHOS off stage; D'ARTAGNAN runs around stage)*

D'ARTAGNAN: *(to audience)* Whew, this is getting tiring!

(enter DUKE)

DUKE: What do you want, D'Artagnan?

D'ARTAGNAN: *(out of breath)* Queen... trouble... necklace... help! *(D'ARTAGNAN hands letter to DUKE)*

DUKE: *(whines)* But, she just gave them to me! *(reads letter)* Trouble... necklace... help! Signed "The Queen". Fine... here are the precious studs! *(hands necklace to D'ARTAGNAN)*

D'ARTAGNAN: Thanks! *(pause, he gasps)* It's missing a couple diamonds!!!!!

DUKE: HUH!? They have been stolen! That darn Milady! She's a sneaky one! *(MILADY sticks her head out from backstage and waves at audience)* But, good thing I made a copy of the necklace. *(hands new necklace to D'ARTAGNAN)* Take this and save the queen! Later!

(MILADY enters)

MILADY: Wait a minute, that wasn't cool.

DUKE: You shouldn't steal, you're a bad person.

(stabs Duke)

DUKE: Ouch! What was that for? You're not supposed to kill me till the end of the play.

MILADY: Yeah, well, we've shortened it a bit. So, goodbye.

DUKE: Goodbye. *(DUKE dies)*

D'ARTAGNAN: NOOOOOOO!!!!

MILADY: YESSSSSSS!!!!

(D'ARTAGNAN grabs MILADY)

D'ARTAGNAN: I'm taking you to the executioner.

MILADY: WHAT? NOOOOOOO!!!!

(D'ARTAGNAN takes MILADY off stage; MILADY screams then re-enters)

MILADY: He just killed me! Well, if I'm going out this way, it's going to be the best death ever! *(dies melodramatically on stage; D'ARTAGNAN enters)*

D'ARTAGNAN: Well, that was overly dramatic.

(MILADY glares at D'ARTAGNAN and then dies again; ALL exit)

ACT 3 SCENE 3

(enter CONSTANCE, D'ARTAGNAN, and QUEEN)

D'ARTAGNAN: Here you go your majesty, your diamonds!

QUEEN: Wow, you rock! And just in time...

(enter KING and CARDINAL with a diabolical smile)

KING: My dear, I see that you have your necklace!

QUEEN: Just for you, my love!

CARDINAL: *(to audience)* MORBLEU!? This really stinks!

KING: What?

CARDINAL: Uhhh, I said, let's all drink! A toast to the queen!

CONSTANCE: Yeah! We saved the day!

D'ARTAGNAN: We sure did! Let's go home!

(ALL exit)

ACT 4 SCENE 1

(D'ARTAGNAN and 3 MUSKETEERS enter)

ARAMIS: D'Artagnan, you have done well, you are now a musketeer!!! *(ARAMIS hands musketeer outfit to D'ARTAGNAN, who cheers)*

ATHOS: Well done! We are now the Four Musketeers!

PORTHOS: But, I thought this story was about the Three Musketeers, you know, us?

ARAMIS: Yeah, but it's really all about D'Artagnan.

PORTHOS: Wait… What!? Why?

ATHOS: Don't know, we didn't write it. But, you know what?

PORTHOS: What?

ATHOS: One for all…

4 MUSKETEERS: And all for one!

(ALL exit)

The End

NOTES

The 20-Minute or so The Three Musketeers

By Alexandre Dumas'
Creatively modified by
Brendan P. Kelso

11-14+ Actors

CAST OF CHARACTERS:

D'ARTAGNAN: Young, arrogant, wannabe musketeer; awesome swordsman

ATHOS: Musketeer #1 – quiet and strong

ARAMIS: Musketeer #2 – quiet and passive

PORTHOS: Musketeer #3 – loud and hungry

CARDINAL RICHELIEU: Our villain and evil mastermind

MILADY de WINTER: Wicked and cunning thief and assassin

KING LOUIS XIII: King of France and not too smart

[1]**QUEEN ANNE:** Queen of France, smarter

[2]**GEORGE VILLIERS, THE DUKE OF BUCKINGHAM:** England; he likes the queen

[3]**MONSIEUR DE TREVILLE:** Captain of the Musketeers

CONSTANCE: D'Artagnan's girlfriend – super cute

COUNT de ROCHEFORT: Cardinal's evil right-hand man

[2]**JUSSAC:** Cardinal's guard and best swordsman in France, until D'Artagnan comes along

[3]**EXECUTIONER:** Uhhh... he kills people

The same actors can play the following parts:
¹Queen and Milady
²Duke and Jussac
³Treville and Executioner

There's a simple pronunciation key for the names and many words throughout the play, located at the back of the book.

ACT 1 SCENE 1

(enter D'ARTAGNAN)

D'ARTAGNAN: *(to audience)* Well, I'm going to travel to Paris to become a Musketeer! I know what you're thinking...that's a great idea! I mean, so what if I'm not even 20 yet, I doubt I'll get in ANY trouble, and hey, I might even find a girl that likes me! Ha, hah, adventure awaits!

(exits)

ACT 1 SCENE 2

(enter D'ARTAGNAN riding a fake horse; enter ROCHEFORT with henchmen)

ROCHEFORT: *(to his henchmen)* That is one ugly horse! *(they all laugh)*

D'ARTAGNAN: Sir, tell me what you are laughing at.

ROCHEFORT: Oh, your horse...very ugly.

D'ARTAGNAN: Don't insult my horse! Let's fight!

ROCHEFORT: Why, my good fellow, you must be mad! *(points behind D'ARTAGNAN)* Oh look, an elephant!

D'ARTAGNAN: Where? *(HENCHMEN intercede and beat up D'ARTAGNAN, he falls to the ground)*

D'ARTAGNAN: Man, that wasn't fair! Who are you?

ROCHEFORT: Ha, hah! Just call me the man of Meung. Goodbye!

(ROCHEFORT exits laughing evilly; D'ARTAGNAN exits holding his head)

ACT 1 SCENE 3

(enter TREVILLE and D'ARTAGNAN)

TREVILLE: I like you D'Artagnan. I myself came to Paris with four crowns. As captain of the Musketeers, I will admit you into the academy and MAYBE, if you're good, in two years you can be a Musketeer!

D'ARTAGNAN: Great! Thank you Monsieur Treville! *(points off stage)* Oh look, it's the man of Meung! I'll get him this time!

(runs off stage; TREVILLE exits)

ACT 1 SCENE 4

(enter 3 MUSKETEERS who stand downstage: ATHOS center; PORTHOS left; ARAMIS right)

ATHOS: *(to audience)* We are the Three Musketeers. I am Athos.

PORTHOS: *(striking a gallant pose)* I am Porthos.

ARAMIS: *(sitting down to read a book)* And I am Aramis.

(enter D'ARTAGNAN)

D'ARTAGNAN: I must catch that man of Meung! *(bumps into ATHOS)* Excuse me, but I am in a hurry.

ATHOS: You are in a hurry?

D'ARTAGNAN: Duh! I'm running across the stage; you are in my way. I did not do it intentionally and I said 'Excuse me.' So, move it buddy, before you get hurt!

ATHOS: Monsieur, you are not polite.

D'ARTAGNAN: I warn you, If I wasn't running after someone... I would....

ATHOS: You would what? Monsieur Man-in-a-hurry, you can find me without running – ME....for a duel. Let's meet at the Carmes-Deschaux. About noon.

D'ARTAGNAN: Where? *(pause)* Whatever! I will be there! Now, out of my way! *(shoves away ATHOS, and runs around stage; ATHOS exits; D'ARTAGNAN runs into PORTHOS and falls to the ground, while PORTHOS doesn't move)*

PORTHOS: Bless me! What do you think you're doing?

D'ARTAGNAN: Excuse me, I was running after someone. *(realizing how big PORTHOS is)* Whoa! You're one big ugly dude....uhhhh, I mean, monsieur.

PORTHOS: What?! Insult me? At one o'clock then, let's duel.

D'ARTAGNAN: Very well, at one o'clock, then. See ya! *(D'ARTAGNAN runs around stage again, PORTHOS exits; ARAMIS gets up, walks across stage and drops handkerchief accidentally from pocket)*

D'ARTAGNAN: Sir! You dropped your handkerchief! *(picks it up)*

ARAMIS: I did not drop it, and it is not mine!

D'ARTAGNAN: What? You have lied twice, monsieur, for I saw it fall from your hands.

ARAMIS: Did you just call me a liar? Well, I will teach you how to behave yourself. Two o'clock. Duel.

D'ARTAGNAN: Really? Sure, why not. Oh, and take your handkerchief, you're going to need it!

(they bow to each other; ARAMIS exits)

D'ARTAGNAN: *(to audience)* Aghhhhhhh!!! Seriously? Three Musketeers in the next three hours!!! But at least, if I am killed, I shall be killed by a Musketeer!

(D'ARTAGNAN exits)

ACT 1 SCENE 5

(ATHOS and D'ARTAGNAN enter)

ATHOS: Glad you could make it. I have engaged two of my friends as seconds.

D'ARTAGNAN: Seconds?

ATHOS: Yeah, they make sure we fight fair. Oh, here they are now!

(enter ARAMIS and PORTHOS singing, "Bad boys, bad boys, whatcha gonna do...")

PORTHOS: Hey! I'm fighting him in an hour. I am going to fight... because...well... I am going to fight!

ARAMIS: And I fight him at two o'clock! Ours is a theological quarrel. *(does a thinking pose)*

D'ARTAGNAN: Yeah, yeah, yeah.... I'll get to you soon!

ATHOS: We are the Three Musketeers; Athos, Porthos, and Aramis.

D'ARTAGNAN: Whatever, Ethos, Pathos, and Logos, let's just finish this! *(swords crossed and are about to fight; enter JUSSAC and cardinal's guards)*

PORTHOS: The cardinal's guards! Sheathe your swords, gentlemen.

JUSSAC: Dueling is illegal! You are under arrest!

ARAMIS: *(to ATHOS and PORTHOS)* There are five of them and we are but three.

D'ARTAGNAN: *(steps forward to join them)* It appears to me we are four! I have the spirit; my heart is that of a Musketeer.

PORTHOS: Great! I love fighting!

(Musketeers say "Fight, fight fight!...Fight, fight, fight!" as they are fighting; D'ARTAGNAN fights JUSSAC and it's the big fight; GUARDS are killed; JUSSAC is wounded and exits; the 3 MUSKETEERS cheer)

ATHOS: Well done! Let's go see the king!

ARAMIS: And we don't have to kill you now!

PORTHOS: And let's get some food, too! I'm hungry!

D'ARTAGNAN: *(to audience)* This is fun!

(ALL exit)

ACT 2 SCENE 1

(enter 3 MUSKETEERS, D'ARTAGNAN, and TREVILLE)

TREVILLE: The king wants to see you, and he's not too happy you killed a few of the cardinal's guards.

(enter KING)

KING: *(yelling)* YOU GUYS HUMILIATED THE CARDINAL'S GUARDS!

ATHOS: Sire, they attacked us!

KING: Oh...Well then, bravo! I hear D'Artagnan beat the cardinal's best swordsman! Brave young man! Here's some money for you. Enjoy! *(hands money to D'ARTAGNAN)*

D'ARTAGNAN: Sweet!

(ALL exit)

ACT 2 SCENE 2

(enter D'ARTAGNAN carrying a message)

D'ARTAGNAN: *(reading letter)* A beautiful maiden has been kidnapped. Her name is Constance and she works for the queen. She was taken by a man with a scar on his face! *(rips letter)* Why, that's my man of Meung! *(yelling out)* I will help find you!

CONSTANCE: *(from off stage)* Thank you!

D'ARTAGNAN: *(yelling out)* Hey Musketeers!

(enter ATHOS, ARAMIS, PORTHOS)

ARAMIS: Hello.

ATHOS: Hello!

PORTHOS: Hello!!!

D'ARTAGNAN: Hello... beautiful girl, vengeance, adventure, going against the cardinal... and possibly even death... you in?

ATHOS: He just said we might die!

PORTHOS: He sure did!

ARAMIS: And we sure might!

3 MUSKETEERS: We're in!

(ALL exit)

ACT 2 SCENE 3

(enter D'ARTAGNAN and CONSTANCE)

D'ARTAGNAN: *(to audience)* There is Constance and wow! I mean like, a whole lot of WOW!

CONSTANCE: Excuse me?

D'ARTAGNAN: Uhhhh... nothing... I mean, you have the sweetest smile in the world!

CONSTANCE: Thanks. *(pause)* Who are you?

D'ARTAGNAN: Oh! I'm D'Artagnan. Your dad asked me to find you, and well, here you are!

CONSTANCE: Right. I just escaped from the cardinal's guards. Now, I must go, because I have some super important stuff to do for the queen!

D'ARTAGNAN: You know what? I like you. No... I LOVE you....

CONSTANCE: Aw, how cute... you're funny. I think I love you too!

(ALL exit)

ACT 2 SCENE 4

(CONSTANCE on stage asleep; DUKE knocks)

CONSTANCE: Who is up at this hour? Can't a girl get her beauty rest?!

(enter DUKE)

DUKE: I am the Duke of Buckingham, and I'm here to see the queen.

CONSTANCE: Buttingham?

DUKE: BUCKINGHAM!!!

CONSTANCE: *(yawning)* Oh... you do realize it is two in the morning.

DUKE: Yes, but knowing our countries hate each other, it's probably best to travel in darkness.

CONSTANCE: Whatever. *(yelling offstage)* Oh, Queen!!!

(enter QUEEN)

DUKE: *(to the QUEEN)* I know you're the Queen of France and I'm from England, but I really, really like you!

QUEEN: Easy there, you're cute and all, but I'm married to the king!

DUKE: Speak on, Queen, the sweetness of your voice is AMAZING! I'm not leaving until you accept my never-ending love for you!

QUEEN: Tell ya what, I'll give you my really beautiful necklace the king gave me IF we never see each other again.

DUKE: Uhhhh, okay.

QUEEN: *(to audience)* I sure hope this doesn't get me in trouble later!

DUKE: *(QUEEN hands necklace to DUKE)* Nice knowing you... but, if you need anything you have my number!

QUEEN: Yeah, yeah...

(ALL exit)

ACT 2 SCENE 5

(enter ROCHEFORT and CARDINAL)

ROCHEFORT: Cardinal Richelieu, our spy informed me she saw the queen with the Duke of Buckingham last night!

CARDINAL: Really? Fantastic!

ROCHEFORT: Yeah, AND the queen gave him a fancy necklace.

CARDINAL: Are you sure of it?

ROCHEFORT: Perfectly sure.

CARDINAL: Well, well! *(ROCHEFORT bows and exits; CARDINAL to audience)* I will use this information and turn the king against the queen. Then, I will take power and rule France! Muahahahahah!!! Now, a special mission. *(calling off stage)* Oh, Milady!!!

(MILADY enters)

MILADY: You called, your eminence?

CARDINAL: Yes. You are a wickedly awesome assassin and thief, and I need you to put those skills to work. Are you up to doing a sinister task?

MILADY: Am I up to it? I am Milady de Winter, the most evil person in this story! You betcha I'm up for it!

CARDINAL: *(to audience)* Wow, she is evil! *(to MILADY)* Please visit the Duke and cut off two diamonds from the queen's necklace.

MILADY: Sounds like fun!

CARDINAL: Awesome, let's laugh evilly while we exit!

MILADY: Yes, let's!

(ALL exit, laughing evilly of course!)

ACT 2 SCENE 6

(enter KING and CARDINAL)

KING: Hello Cardinal, what are you laughing about?

CARDINAL: Oh, nothing. How are you?

KING: Couldn't be better!

CARDINAL: Oh... well... that's good.

KING: Why do you say that?

CARDINAL: Well...no...it's not my place.

KING: What? I must know!

CARDINAL: Well sire, it seems that Buckingham has been in Paris five days.

KING: Buckingham in Paris!!! MORDIEU! But, we are enemies! What was he doing here?

CARDINAL: Yeah, about that, rumor has it...no, no... it's too much, sire.

KING: I am the king! You must tell me.

CARDINAL: Your Highness, it seems that he spoke with the queen last night.

KING: No, PARDIEU, no! My wife? But why?

CARDINAL: Well, the Duke IS handsome and powerful, but that can't have ANYTHING to do with it, right?

KING: You think that she deceives me?!

CARDINAL: What?! Nooooo... well...maybe? *(winking to audience)*

KING: What should I do?

CARDINAL: Not sure. *(pause)* Oh, I know, maybe you should show her how faithful you are and throw a big party for her!

KING: How fun!

CARDINAL: Oh, and you can ask her to wear those beautiful diamonds which you gave her, as a token of her love.

KING: Yes, yes, this is good. I'm glad I thought of this! I will tell her right now! *(to audience)* I love it when I come up with great ideas! *(KING exits)*

CARDINAL: *(to audience)* Wow, he's a doofus… taking over power and ruling France will be MUCH easier than I thought! Muahahahah!!!!!

(CARDINAL exits)

ACT 2 SCENE 7

(enter KING, QUEEN, and CONSTANCE)

KING: To show my undying love. I'm throwing a party next week, just for YOU!

QUEEN: That's fantastic! I'm so happy!

KING: And above all, can you wear that beautiful necklace I gave you?

QUEEN: *(to audience)* Uh, oh!

KING: What?

QUEEN: Uhhh, I said, I can't wait to go! So excited!

KING: Great! See ya later! *(KING exits)*

QUEEN: Oh, no! I am lost! I am lost! I just gave that necklace to the Duke!

CONSTANCE: Wait! I have an idea! I'll have my new love, D'Artagnan, and his friends, get your necklace back.

QUEEN: Awesome! I'm so happy again!

(ALL exit)

ACT 3 SCENE 1

(enter D'ARTAGNAN, CONSTANCE, and 3 MUSKETEERS)

CONSTANCE: D'Artagnan, I need you to go to England, get the queen's necklace back from the Duke, and return it within the next two scenes, or the queen will DIE!

ARAMIS: Wow, no pressure.

PORTHOS: This will be fun!

D'ARTAGNAN: So, are you guys in?

ATHOS: One for all, and all for one – That is our motto, is it not?

D'ARTAGNAN: Yes!

(they put their swords together)

ALL: One for all, and all for one!

(ALL exit running off stage)

ACT 3 SCENE 2

(enter D'ARTAGNAN and 3 MUSKETEERS)

PORTHOS: Well men, this journey should be pretty easy!

(enter cardinal's guards)

ARAMIS: Uhhhh, what did you just say?

PORTHOS: Well, it may be a bit harder than I thought! Go on without me, I'll fight them off! FOR FRANCE!!! *(Says, "fight, fight, fight..."; PORTHOS starts fighting them; PORTHOS kills one while the others run; PORTHOS chases them off stage)*

(D'ARTAGNAN, ARAMIS, and ATHOS run around stage)

ARAMIS: Well, we are getting close.

(CARDINAL'S GUARDS sneak up behind D'ARTAGNAN, ARAMIS, and ATHOS. They start attacking; fight breaks out; everyone saying, "fight, fight, fight..."; GUARDS are killed; ARAMIS is hurt)

ATHOS: Aramis, you're hurt!

ARAMIS: It's just a flesh wound! But, I can proceed no farther! I'll hold off any others!

(ARAMIS exits; ATHOS and D'ARTAGNAN run around stage; 3 GUARDS sneak up behind ATHOS and capture him)

D'ARTAGNAN: Athos!

ATHOS: Go on D'Artagnan! Besides, there's only three of them, I've got this! *(GUARDS take ATHOS off stage; D'ARTAGNAN runs around stage)*

D'ARTAGNAN: *(to audience)* Whew, this is getting tiring!

(enter DUKE)

DUKE: What do you want, D'Artagnan?

D'ARTAGNAN: *(out of breath)* Queen... trouble... necklace... help! *(D'ARTAGNAN hands letter to DUKE)*

DUKE: *(whines)* But, she just gave them to me! *(reads letter)* Trouble... necklace... help! Signed "The Queen". Fine... here are the precious studs! *(hands necklace to D'ARTAGNAN)*

D'ARTAGNAN: Thanks! *(pause, he gasps)* It's missing a couple diamonds!!!!!

DUKE: HUH!? They have been stolen! That darn Milady! She's a sneaky one! *(MILADY sticks her head out from backstage and waves at audience)* But, good thing I made a copy of the necklace. *(hands new necklace to D'ARTAGNAN)* Take this and save the queen! Later!

(MILADY enters)

MILADY: Wait a minute, that wasn't cool.

DUKE: You shouldn't steal, you're a bad person.

(stabs Duke)

DUKE: Ouch! What was that for? You're not supposed to kill me till the end of the play.

MILADY: Yeah, well, we've shortened it a bit. So, goodbye.

DUKE: Goodbye. *(DUKE dies)*

D'ARTAGNAN: NOOOOOOO!!!!

MILADY: YESSSSSSS!!!!

(D'ARTAGNAN grabs MILADY)

D'ARTAGNAN: I'm taking you to the executioner.

MILADY: WHAT? NOOOOOOO!!!!

D'ARTAGNAN: Oh, executioner!!!

(enter EXECUTIONER)

EXECUTIONER: You called?

D'ARTAGNAN: Yep. *(pointing at MILADY)* Bad, bad, lady…. You know what to do.

EXECUTIONER: Yep! *(takes MILADY off stage; MILADY screams then re-enters)*

MILADY: He just killed me! Well, if I'm going out this way, it's going to be the best death ever! *(dies melodramatically on stage)*

D'ARTAGNAN: Well, that was overly dramatic.

(MILADY glares at D'ARTAGNAN and then dies again; ALL exit)

ACT 3 SCENE 3

(enter CONSTANCE, D'ARTAGNAN, and QUEEN)

D'ARTAGNAN: Here you go your majesty, your diamonds!

QUEEN: Wow, you rock! And just in time…

(enter KING, TREVILLE, and CARDINAL with a diabolical smile)

KING: My dear, I see that you have your necklace!

QUEEN: Just for you, my love!

CARDINAL: *(to audience)* MORBLEU!? This really stinks!

TREVILLE: What?

CARDINAL: Uhhh, I said, let's all drink! A toast to the queen!

CONSTANCE: Yeah! We saved the day!

D'ARTAGNAN: We sure did! Let's go home!

(ALL exit)

ACT 4 SCENE 1

(D'ARTAGNAN, TREVILLE, and 3 MUSKETEERS enter)

TREVILLE: D'Artagnan, you have done well, you are now a musketeer!!! *(TREVILLE hands musketeer outfit to D'ARTAGNAN, who cheers)*

ATHOS: Well done! We are now the Four Musketeers!

PORTHOS: But, I thought this story was about the Three Musketeers, you know, us?

ARAMIS: Yeah, but it's really all about D'Artagnan.

PORTHOS: Wait... What!? Why?

ATHOS: Don't know, we didn't write it. But, you know what?

PORTHOS: What?

ATHOS: One for all...

4 MUSKETEERS: And all for one!

(ALL exit)

The End

The 25-Minute or so The Three Musketeers

By Alexandre Dumas'
Creatively modified by
Brendan P. Kelso

12-17+ Actors

CAST OF CHARACTERS:

D'ARTAGNAN: Young, arrogant, wannabe musketeer; awesome swordsman

ATHOS: Musketeer #1 – quiet and strong

ARAMIS: Musketeer #2 – quiet and passive

PORTHOS: Musketeer #3 – loud, hungry, and not as smart as the other two

CARDINAL RICHELIEU: Our villain and evil mastermind

[2]**MILADY de WINTER:** Wicked and cunning thief and assassin

[1]**KING LOUIS XIII:** King of France and not too smart

[2]**QUEEN ANNE:** Queen of France, smarter

[3]**GEORGE VILLIERS, THE DUKE OF BUCKINGHAM:** England; he likes the queen

[4]**MONSIEUR DE TREVILLE:** Captain of the Musketeers

CONSTANCE: D'Artagnan's girlfriend – super cute

COUNT de ROCHEFORT: Cardinal's evil right-hand man

[1]**M. D'ARTAGNAN:** D'Artagnan's dad and retired Musketeer

[5]**MONSIEUR BONACIEUX:** Constance's dad

[3]**PLANCHET:** Servant of D'Artagnan

[5]**JUSSAC:** Cardinal's guard and best swordsman in France, until D'Artagnan comes along

[4]**EXECUTIONER:** Uhhh... he kills people

The same actors can play the following parts:
[1] King and M. D'Artagnan
[2] Queen and Milady
[3] Duke and Planchet
[4] Treville and Executioner
[5] Jussac and Bonacieux
extra actors can be various guards and henchmen

There's a simple pronunciation key for the names and many words throughout the play, located at the back of the book.

ACT 1 SCENE 1

(enter D'ARTAGNAN and MONSIEUR D'ARTAGNAN)

D'ARTAGNAN: Dad, I'm going to travel to Paris to become a Musketeer!

M. D'ARTAGNAN: D'Artagnan, that's a great idea! I mean you're not even 20 yet, so yeah, runoff where nobody knows you, you'll probably be killed by the end of the first act, and you might even find a girl that likes you! Ha, hah, adventure awaits!

D'ARTAGNAN: Yeah, that's exactly what I was thinking!

M. D'ARTAGNAN: Take our trusty old horse and remember, never fear quarrels, but seek adventures! *(M. D'ARTAGNAN hands D'ARTAGNAN a fake ugly horse)*

D'ARTAGNAN: Thanks, Dad! *(D'ARTAGNAN exits)*

M. D'ARTAGNAN: Bye! *(to audience)* Teenagers!

(exits)

ACT 1 SCENE 2

(enter D'ARTAGNAN riding a fake horse; enter ROCHEFORT with henchmen)

ROCHEFORT: *(to his henchmen)* That is one ugly horse! *(they all laugh)*

D'ARTAGNAN: Sir, tell me what you are laughing at.

ROCHEFORT: Oh, your horse...very ugly.

D'ARTAGNAN: Don't insult my horse! Let's fight!

ROCHEFORT: Why, my good fellow, you must be mad! *(points behind D'ARTAGNAN)* Oh look, an elephant!

D'ARTAGNAN: Where? *(HENCHMEN intercede and beat up D'ARTAGNAN, he falls to the ground)*

D'ARTAGNAN: Man, that wasn't fair! Who are you?

ROCHEFORT: Ha, hah! Just call me the man of Meung. Goodbye! *(ROCHEFORT exits laughing evilly; D'ARTAGNAN exits holding his head)*

ACT 1 SCENE 3

(enter TREVILLE and D'ARTAGNAN)

TREVILLE: I like you D'Artagnan. I myself came to Paris with four crowns. As captain of the Musketeers, I will admit you into the academy and MAYBE, if you're good, in two years you can be a Musketeer!

D'ARTAGNAN: Great! Thank you Monsieur Treville! *(points off stage)* Oh look, it's the man of Meung! I'll get him this time!

(runs off stage; TREVILLE exits)

ACT 1 SCENE 4

(enter 3 MUSKETEERS who stand downstage: ATHOS center; PORTHOS left; ARAMIS right)

ATHOS: *(to audience)* We are the Three Musketeers. I am Athos.

PORTHOS: *(striking a gallant pose)* I am Porthos.

ARAMIS: *(sitting down to read a book)* And I am Aramis.

(enter D'ARTAGNAN)

D'ARTAGNAN: I must catch that man of Meung! *(bumps into ATHOS)* Excuse me, but I am in a hurry.

ATHOS: You are in a hurry?

D'ARTAGNAN: Duh! I'm running across the stage; you are in my way. I did not do it intentionally and I said 'Excuse me.' So, move it buddy, before you get hurt!

ATHOS: Monsieur, you are not polite.

D'ARTAGNAN: I warn you, If I wasn't running after someone... I would....

ATHOS: You would what? Monsieur Man-in-a-hurry, you can find me without running – ME....for a duel. Let's meet at the Carmes-Deschaux. About noon.

D'ARTAGNAN: Where? *(pause)* Whatever! I will be there! Now, out of my way! *(shoves away ATHOS, and runs around stage; ATHOS exits; D'ARTAGNAN runs into PORTHOS and falls to the ground, while PORTHOS doesn't move)*

PORTHOS: Bless me! What do you think you're doing?

D'ARTAGNAN: Excuse me, I was running after someone. *(realizing how big PORTHOS is)* Whoa! You're one big ugly dude….uhhhh, I mean, monsieur.

PORTHOS: What?! Insult me? At one o'clock then, let's duel.

D'ARTAGNAN: Very well, at one o'clock, then. See ya! *(D'ARTAGNAN runs around stage again, PORTHOS exits; ARAMIS gets up, walks across stage and drops handkerchief accidentally from pocket)*

D'ARTAGNAN: Sir! You dropped your handkerchief! *(picks it up)*

ARAMIS: I did not drop it, and it is not mine!

D'ARTAGNAN: What? You have lied twice, monsieur, for I saw it fall from your hands.

ARAMIS: Did you just call me a liar? Well, I will teach you how to behave yourself. Two o'clock. Duel.

D'ARTAGNAN: Really? Sure, why not. Oh, and take your handkerchief, you're going to need it!

(they bow to each other; ARAMIS exits)

D'ARTAGNAN: *(to audience)* Aghhhhhhh!!! Seriously? Three Musketeers in the next three hours!!! But at least, if I am killed, I shall be killed by a Musketeer!

(D'ARTAGNAN exits)

ACT 1 SCENE 5

(ATHOS and D'ARTAGNAN enter)

ATHOS: Glad you could make it. I have engaged two of my friends as seconds.

D'ARTAGNAN: Seconds?

ATHOS: Yeah, they make sure we fight fair. Oh, here they are now!

(enter ARAMIS and PORTHOS singing, "Bad boys, bad boys, whatcha gonna do...")

PORTHOS: Hey! I'm fighting him in an hour. I am going to fight... because...well... I am going to fight!

ARAMIS: And I fight him at two o'clock! Ours is a theological quarrel. *(does a thinking pose)*

D'ARTAGNAN: Yeah, yeah, yeah.... I'll get to you soon!

ATHOS: We are the Three Musketeers; Athos, Porthos, and Aramis.

D'ARTAGNAN: Whatever, Ethos, Pathos, and Logos, let's just finish this! *(swords crossed and are about to fight; enter JUSSAC and cardinal's guards)*

PORTHOS: The cardinal's guards! Sheathe your swords, gentlemen.

JUSSAC: Dueling is illegal! You are under arrest!

ARAMIS: *(to ATHOS and PORTHOS)* There are five of them and we are but three.

D'ARTAGNAN: *(steps forward to join them)* It appears to me we are four! I have the spirit; my heart is that of a Musketeer.

PORTHOS: Great! I love fighting!

(Musketeers say "Fight, fight fight!...Fight, fight, fight!" as they are fighting; GUARDS are killed; D'ARTAGNAN fights JUSSAC and it's the big fight; JUSSAC is wounded and exits; the 3 MUSKETEERS cheer)

ATHOS: Well done! Let's go see Treville and the king!

ARAMIS: And we don't have to kill you now!

PORTHOS: And let's get some food, too! I'm hungry!

D'ARTAGNAN: *(to audience)* This is fun!

(ALL exit)

ACT 2 SCENE 1

(enter 3 MUSKETEERS, D'ARTAGNAN, and TREVILLE)

TREVILLE: The king wants to see you, and he's not too happy you killed a few of the cardinal's guards.

(enter KING)

KING: *(yelling)* YOU GUYS HUMILIATED THE CARDINAL'S GUARDS!

ATHOS: Sire, they attacked us!

KING: Oh…Well then, bravo! I hear D'Artagnan beat the cardinal's best swordsman! Brave young man! Here's some money for you. Enjoy! *(hands money to D'ARTAGNAN)*

D'ARTAGNAN: Sweet!

(ALL exit)

ACT 2 SCENE 2

(enter D'ARTAGNAN and PLANCHET)

PLANCHET: *(to audience)* Hello, I'm Planchet. I'm D'Artagnan's servant.

(enter MONSIEUR BONACIEUX)

BONACIEUX: Sir! I need your help, desperately!!!

PLANCHET: *(stepping forward)* What do you want?

BONACIEUX: My daughter has been kidnapped. Her name is Constance and she works for the queen. She was taken by a man with a scar on his face!

D'ARTAGNAN: Why, that's my man of Meung! *(to BONACIEUX)* We will help you find her! *(yells offstage)* Hey Musketeers!

(enter ATHOS, ARAMIS, PORTHOS)

ARAMIS: Hello.

ATHOS: Hello!

PORTHOS: Hello!!!

D'ARTAGNAN: Hello... beautiful girl, vengeance, adventure, going against the cardinal... and possibly even death... you in?

ATHOS: He just said we might die!

PORTHOS: He sure did!

ARAMIS: And we sure might!

3 MUSKETEERS: We're in!

(ALL exit)

ACT 2 SCENE 3

(enter D'ARTAGNAN and CONSTANCE)

D'ARTAGNAN: *(to audience)* There is Constance and wow! I mean like, a whole lot of **WOW!**

CONSTANCE: Excuse me?

D'ARTAGNAN: Uhhhh... nothing... I mean, you have the sweetest smile in the world!

CONSTANCE: Thanks. *(pause)* Who are you?

D'ARTAGNAN: Oh! I'm D'Artagnan. Your dad asked me to find you, and well, here you are!

CONSTANCE: Right. I just escaped from the cardinal's guards. Now, I must go, because I have some super important stuff to do for the queen!

D'ARTAGNAN: You know what? I like you. No... I LOVE you....

CONSTANCE: Aw, how cute... you're funny. I think I love you too!

(ALL exit)

ACT 2 SCENE 4

(CONSTANCE on stage asleep; DUKE knocks)

CONSTANCE: Who is up at this hour? Can't a girl get her beauty rest?!

(enter DUKE)

DUKE: I am the Duke of Buckingham, and I'm here to see the queen.

CONSTANCE: Buttingham?

DUKE: BUCKINGHAM!!!

CONSTANCE: *(yawning)* Oh... you do realize it is two in the morning.

DUKE: Yes, but knowing our countries hate each other, it's probably best to travel in darkness.

CONSTANCE: Whatever. *(yelling offstage)* Oh, Queen!!!

(enter QUEEN)

DUKE: *(to the QUEEN)* I know you're the Queen of France and I'm from England, but I really, really like you!

QUEEN: Easy there, you're cute and all, but I'm married to the king!

DUKE: Speak on, Queen, the sweetness of your voice is AMAZING! I'm not leaving until you accept my never-ending love for you!

QUEEN: Tell ya what, I'll give you my really beautiful necklace the king gave me IF we never see each other again.

DUKE: Uhhhh, okay.

QUEEN: *(to audience)* I sure hope this doesn't get me in trouble later!

DUKE: *(QUEEN hands necklace to DUKE)* Nice knowing you… but, if you need anything you have my number!

QUEEN: Yeah, yeah…

(ALL exit)

ACT 2 SCENE 5

(enter ROCHEFORT and CARDINAL)

ROCHEFORT: Cardinal Richelieu, our spy informed me she saw the queen with the Duke of Buckingham last night!

CARDINAL: Really? Fantastic!

ROCHEFORT: Yeah, AND the queen gave him a fancy necklace.

CARDINAL: Are you sure of it?

ROCHEFORT: Perfectly sure.

CARDINAL: Well, well! *(ROCHEFORT bows and exits; CARDINAL to audience)* I will use this information and turn the king against the queen. Then, I will take power and rule France! Muahahahahah!!! Now, a special mission. *(calling off stage)* Oh, Milady!!!

(MILADY enters)

MILADY: You called, your eminence?

CARDINAL: Yes. You are a wickedly awesome assassin and thief, and I need you to put those skills to work. Are you up to doing a sinister task?

MILADY: Am I up to it? I am Milady de Winter, the most evil person in this story! You betcha I'm up for it!

CARDINAL: *(to audience)* Wow, she is evil! *(to MILADY)* Please visit the Duke and cut off two diamonds from the queen's necklace.

MILADY: Sounds like fun!

CARDINAL: Awesome, let's laugh evilly while we exit!

MILADY: Yes, let's!

(ALL exit, laughing evilly of course!)

ACT 2 SCENE 6

(enter KING and CARDINAL)

KING: Hello Cardinal, what are you laughing about?

CARDINAL: Oh, nothing. How are you?

KING: Couldn't be better!

CARDINAL: Oh... well... that's good.

KING: Why do you say that?

CARDINAL: Well...no...it's not my place.

KING: What? I must know!

CARDINAL: Well sire, it seems that Buckingham has been in Paris five days.

KING: Buckingham in Paris!!! MORDIEU! But, we are enemies! What was he doing here?

CARDINAL: Yeah, about that, rumor has it...no, no... it's too much, sire.

KING: I am the king! You must tell me.

CARDINAL: Your Highness, it seems that he spoke with the queen last night.

KING: No, PARDIEU, no! My wife? But why?

CARDINAL: Well, the Duke IS handsome and powerful, but that can't have ANYTHING to do with it, right?

KING: You think that she deceives me?!

CARDINAL: What?! Nooooo... well...maybe? *(winking to audience)*

KING: What should I do?

CARDINAL: Not sure. *(pause)* Oh, I know, maybe you should show her how faithful you are and throw a big party for her!

KING: How fun!

CARDINAL: Oh, and you can ask her to wear those beautiful diamonds which you gave her, as a token of her love.

KING: Yes, yes, this is good. I'm glad I thought of this! I will tell her right now! *(to audience)* I love it when I come up with great ideas! *(KING exits)*

CARDINAL: *(to audience)* Wow, he's a doofus... taking over power and ruling France will be MUCH easier than I thought! Muahahahah!!!!!

(CARDINAL exits)

ACT 2 SCENE 7

(enter KING, QUEEN, and CONSTANCE)

KING: To show my undying love, I'm throwing a party next week, just for YOU!

QUEEN: That's fantastic! I'm so happy!

KING: And above all, can you wear that beautiful necklace I gave you?

QUEEN: *(to audience)* Uh, oh!

KING: What?

QUEEN: Uhhh, I said, I can't wait to go! So excited!

KING: Great! See ya later! *(KING exits)*

QUEEN: Oh, no! I am lost! I am lost! I just gave that necklace to the Duke!

CONSTANCE: Wait! I have an idea! I'll have my new love, D'Artagnan, and his friends, get your necklace back.

QUEEN: Awesome! I'm so happy again!

(ALL exit)

ACT 3 SCENE 1

(enter D'ARTAGNAN, CONSTANCE, and 3 MUSKETEERS)

CONSTANCE: D'Artagnan, I need you to go to England, get the queen's necklace back from the Duke, and return it within the next two scenes, or the queen will DIE!

ARAMIS: Wow, no pressure.

PORTHOS: This will be fun!

D'ARTAGNAN: So, are you guys in?

ATHOS: One for all, and all for one – That is our motto, is it not?

D'ARTAGNAN: Yes!

(they put their swords together)

ALL: One for all, and all for one!

(ALL exit running off stage)

ACT 3 SCENE 2

(enter D'ARTAGNAN and 3 MUSKETEERS)

PORTHOS: Well men, this journey should be pretty easy!

(enter cardinal's guards)

ARAMIS: Uhhhh, what did you just say?

PORTHOS: Well, it may be a bit harder than I thought! Go on without me, I'll fight them off! FOR FRANCE!!! *(Says, "fight, fight, fight..."; PORTHOS starts fighting them; PORTHOS kills one while the others run; PORTHOS chases them off stage)*

(D'ARTAGNAN, ARAMIS, and ATHOS run around stage)

ARAMIS: Well, we are getting close.

(CARDINAL'S GUARDS sneak up behind D'ARTAGNAN, ARAMIS, and ATHOS. They start attacking; fight breaks out; everyone saying, "fight, fight, fight..."; GUARDS are killed; ARAMIS is hurt)

ATHOS: Aramis, you're hurt!

ARAMIS: It's just a flesh wound! But, I can proceed no farther! I'll hold off any others!

(ARAMIS exits; ATHOS and D'ARTAGNAN run around stage; 3 GUARDS sneak up behind ATHOS and capture him)

D'ARTAGNAN: Athos!

ATHOS: Go on D'Artagnan! Besides, there's only three of them, I've got this! *(GUARDS take ATHOS off stage; D'ARTAGNAN runs around stage)*

D'ARTAGNAN: *(to audience)* Whew, this is getting tiring!

(enter DUKE)

DUKE: What do you want, D'Artagnan?

D'ARTAGNAN: *(out of breath)* Queen... trouble... necklace... help! *(D'ARTAGNAN hands letter to DUKE)*

DUKE: *(whines)* But, she just gave them to me! *(reads letter)* Trouble... necklace... help! Signed "The Queen". Fine... here are the precious studs! *(hands necklace to D'ARTAGNAN)*

D'ARTAGNAN: Thanks! *(pause, he gasps)* It's missing a couple diamonds!!!!!

DUKE: HUH!? They have been stolen! That darn Milady! She's a sneaky one! *(MILADY sticks her head out from backstage and waves at audience)* But, good thing I made a copy of the necklace. *(hands new necklace to D'ARTAGNAN)* Take this and save the queen! Later!

(MILADY enters)

MILADY: Wait a minute, that wasn't cool.

DUKE: You shouldn't steal, you're a bad person.

(stabs Duke)

DUKE: Ouch! What was that for? You're not supposed to kill me till the end of the play.

MILADY: Yeah, well, we've shortened it a bit. So, goodbye.

DUKE: Goodbye. *(DUKE dies)*

D'ARTAGNAN: NOOOOOOO!!!!

MILADY: YESSSSSSS!!!!

(D'ARTAGNAN grabs MILADY)

D'ARTAGNAN: I'm taking you to the executioner.

MILADY: WHAT? NOOOOOOO!!!!

D'ARTAGNAN: Oh, executioner!!!

(enter EXECUTIONER)

EXECUTIONER: You called?

D'ARTAGNAN: Yep. *(pointing at MILADY)* Bad, bad, lady…. You know what to do.

EXECUTIONER: Yep! *(takes MILADY off stage; MILADY screams then re-enters)*

MILADY: He just killed me! Well, if I'm going out this way, it's going to be the best death ever! *(dies melodramatically on stage)*

D'ARTAGNAN: Well, that was overly dramatic.

(MILADY glares at D'ARTAGNAN and then dies again; ALL exit)

ACT 3 SCENE 3

(enter CONSTANCE, D'ARTAGNAN, and QUEEN)

D'ARTAGNAN: Here you go your majesty, your diamonds!

QUEEN: Wow, you rock! And just in time...

(enter KING, TREVILLE, and CARDINAL with a diabolical smile)

KING: My dear, I see that you have your necklace!

QUEEN: Just for you, my love!

CARDINAL: *(to audience)* MORBLEU!? This really stinks!

TREVILLE: What?

CARDINAL: Uhhh, I said, let's all drink! A toast to the queen!

CONSTANCE: Yeah! We saved the day!

D'ARTAGNAN: We sure did! Let's go home!

(ALL exit)

ACT 4 SCENE 1

(D'ARTAGNAN, TREVILLE, and 3 MUSKETEERS enter)

TREVILLE: D'Artagnan, you have done well, you are now a musketeer!!! *(TREVILLE hands musketeer outfit to D'ARTAGNAN, who cheers)*

ATHOS: Well done! We are now the Four Musketeers!

PORTHOS: But, I thought this story was about the Three Musketeers, you know, us?

ARAMIS: Yeah, but it's really all about D'Artagnan.

PORTHOS: Wait... What!? Why?

ATHOS: Don't know, we didn't write it. But, you know what?

PORTHOS: What?

ATHOS: One for all...

4 MUSKETEERS: And all for one!

(ALL exit)

The End

PRONUNCIATION KEY
Simplified for easy pronunciations

Bonacieux: Bon-a-sue
Carmes-Deschaux: Karm-de-sho
Carte Blanche: Kart blah-nsh
D'Artagnan: Dar-tan-yan
Fleur-de-lis: Flur-de-lees
Jussac: Juice-ack
Livre: Lee-vra
MiLady: Mi-lady
Moi: Muah
Monsieur: Mi-sur
Morbleu: More-blue
Mordieu: More-du
Pardieu: Par-du
Planchet: Plan-shay
Richelieu: Rish-uh-lu
Rochefort: Rosh-four
Sacre bleu: Sa-kray-blue
Treville: Tray-vil

SPECIAL THANKS

As with all books that I write, it takes a team. When I first starting writing these books, it was just me and a dream. Now, I have many different individuals that are willing to help out in the creative process and I wanted to send them a little love.

To all of my script reviewers: First of all, my wife and kid! As well as, Kenny, Ian Campbell, Suzy Newman, Khara C. Barnhart, Angi, Eli, Holli, Jean, Ben and Bradley, Sandra, Ginger & family, and Amy, thank you so very much! This book would not be near as funny without your witticisms!!!

Sandra, thank you so much for being my on the fly editor! I still don't quite understand king and King - but, I'm glad you do!

Sneak Peeks at other Playing With Plays books:

Richard III for Kids .... Pg 81

Treasure Island for Kids .... Pg 84

Henry V for Kids .... Pg 86

King Lear for Kids .... Pg 89

Two Gentlemen of Verona for Kids .... Pg 92

Christmas Carol for Kids .... Pg 95

Tempest for Kids .... Pg 97

Hamlet for Kids .... Pg 100

Sneak peek of
Richard III for Kids
ACT 1 SCENE 4

(CLARENCE is in prison, sleeping; he wakes up from a bad dream)

CLARENCE: Terrible, horrible, no good, very bad dream! *(pauses, notices audience and addresses them)* O, I have pass'd a miserable night! I dreamt that Richard was trying to kill me! Hahahaha, Richard is SUCH a good guy, he would NEVER do a thing like that!

(enter MURDERER carrying a weapon)

MURDERER: I sounded like such a pro, no one will know it's my first day on the job! Hehehe!

CLARENCE: Hey! Who's there?

MURDERER: Um... um... *(hides his murder weapon behind his back)*

CLARENCE: Your eyes do menace me. Are you planning to murder me? 'Cause that's not a good idea. My brother Richard is a REALLY powerful guy.

MURDERER: Ha! Richard is the one who sent me here to do this! *(a pause)* Whoops...

CLARENCE: Hahaha, you foolish fellow. Richard loves me.

MURDERER: Dude, what are you not getting? He PAID me to do this!

CLARENCE: O, do not slander him, for he is kind.

(The MURDERER stabs CLARENCE; CLARENCE dies a dramatic death)

CLARENCE: Kinda ruthless... *(dies)*

MURDERER: *(Gasps)* Oh, my! He's dead! I feel bad now... I bet Clarence was a really nice guy. Ahhh, the guilt! Wow, I should have stayed in clown school.

(MURDERER exits)

ACT 2 SCENE 1

(KING EDWARD is surrounded by QUEEN ELIZABETH and BUCKINGHAM)

KING EDWARD: Well, this has been a great day at work! Everyone's agreed to get along!

(ELIZABETH and BUCKINGHAM shake hands with each other to celebrate the peace; enter RICHARD; KING EDWARD smiles happily)

KING EDWARD: If I die, I will be at peace! But I must say I'm feeling a lot healthier after all of this peace-making!

RICHARD: Hey! Looks like you're all in a good mood. That's great, 'cause you know I LOVE getting along! So what's up?

KING EDWARD: I made them like each other!

RICHARD: How lovely! I like you all now, too! Group hug? *(everyone shakes their head)* No? *(he grins sweetly)*

ELIZABETH: Wonderful! Once Clarence gets back from the Tower, everything will be perfect!

RICHARD: WHAT??? We make peace and then you insult us like this? That's no way to talk about a DEAD man!!

(EVERYONE gasps)

KING EDWARD: Is Clarence dead? I told them to cancel the execution!

RICHARD: Oh, yeah… guess that was too late! *(winks to audience)*

KING EDWARD: Nooooooo!!!! Oh my poor brother! Now I feel more sick than EVER! Oh, poor Clarence!

(All exit except RICHARD and BUCKINGHAM)

RICHARD: Well, that sure worked as planned!

BUCKINGHAM: Great job, partner!

(both exit, laughing evilly)

Sneak peek of
Treasure Island for Kids

(enter JIM, TRELAWNEY, and DOCTOR; enter CAPTAIN SMOLLETT from the other side of the stage)

TRELAWNEY: Hello Captain. Are we all shipshape and seaworthy?

CAPTAIN: Trelawney, I don't know what you're thinking, but I don't like this cruise; and I don't like the men.

TRELAWNEY: *(very angry)* Perhaps you don't like the ship?

CAPTAIN: Nope, I said it short and sweet.

DOCTOR: What? Why?

CAPTAIN: Because I heard we are going on a treasure hunt and the coordinates of the island are: *(whispers to DOCTOR)*

DOCTOR: Wow! That's exactly right!

CAPTAIN: There's been too much blabbing already.

DOCTOR: Right! But, I doubt ANYTHING will go wrong!

CAPTAIN: Fine. Let's sail!

(ALL exit)

Act 2 Scene 3

(enter JIM, SILVER, and various other pirates)

SILVER: Ay, ay, mates. You know the song: Fifteen men on the dead man's chest.

ALL PIRATES: Yo-ho-ho and a bottle of rum!

(PIRATES slowly exit)

JIM: *(to the audience)* So, the Hispaniola had begun her voyage to the Isle of Treasure. As for Long John, well, he still is the nicest cook...

SILVER: Do you want a sandwich?

JIM: That would be great, thanks Long John! *(SILVER exits; JIM addresses audience)* As you can see, Long John is a swell guy! Until...

(JIM hides in the corner)

Act 2 Scene 4

(enter SILVER and OTHER PIRATES)

JIM: *(to audience)* I overheard Long John talking to the rest of the pirates.

SILVER: Listen here you, Scallywags! I was with Captain Flint when he hid this treasure. And those cowards have the map. Follow my directions, and no killing, yet. Clear?

DICK: Clear.

SILVER: But, when we do kill them, I claim Trelawney. And remember, dead men don't bite.

GEORGE: Ay, ay, Long John!

(ALL exit but JIM)

JIM: *(to audience)* Oh no! Long John Silver IS the one-legged man that Billy Bones warned me about! I have to tell the others!

(JIM runs offstage)

Sneak peek of
Henry V for Kids
ACT 2 SCENE 2

(enter BEDFORD and EXETER, observing CAMBRIDGE and SCROOP, who whisper among themselves)

BEDFORD: Hey Exeter, do you think it's a good idea that King Henry is letting those conspirators wander around freely?

EXETER: It's alright, Bedford. King Henry has a plan! He knows EVERYTHING they are plotting. BUT, they don't KNOW he knows. And HE knows that they don't know he knows...and...

BEDFORD: *(interrupting)* Okay, okay, I get it. Let's go sit in the audience and watch! *(they sit in the audience; enter HENRY)*

HENRY: Greetings, my good and FAITHFUL friends, Cambridge and Scroop. Perfect timing! I need your advice on something.

CAMBRIDGE: Sure thing. You know we'd do anything for you! Never was a monarch better feared and loved.

SCROOP: That's why we're going to kick some French butt!! *(SCROOP and CAMBRIDGE high-five)*

HENRY: Excellent! A man was arrested yesterday for shouting nasty things about me. But I'm sure by now he's thought better of it. I think I ought to show mercy and pardon him.

SCROOP: Nah, let him be punished.

HENRY: Ahhh, but let us yet be merciful.

CAMBRIDGE: Nah, I'm with Scroop! Off with his head!

HENRY: Is that your final answer?

CAMBRIDGE & SCROOP: YES!

HENRY: Ok, but if we don't show mercy for small offenses, how will we show mercy for big ones? I will release him. Now, take a look at THESE LETTERS.

(as CAMBRIDGE and SCROOP read the letters, their jaws drop)

HENRY: Why, how now, gentlemen? What see you in those papers that your jaws hang so low?

EXETER: *(to audience)* The letters betray their guilt!

CAMBRIDGE: I do confess my fault...

SCROOP: ...and do submit me to your Highness' mercy! *(they start begging and pleading on the ground)*

HENRY: Exeter, Bedford, arrest these traitors. What did they say... Oh yeah, OFF WITH THEIR HEADS!

CAMBRIDGE: Whoa there!

SCROOP: Off with our what? What happened to the whole "mercy" thing you were just talking about!?

HENRY: Your own words talked me out of it! Take them away!

CAMBRIDGE: Well, this stinks!

(EXETER and BEDFORD arrest CAMBRIDGE and SCROOP; ALL exit, except HENRY)

HENRY: Being king is no fun sometimes. Scroop used to be one of my best friends. *(SCROOP runs on stage and dies melodramatically)* But there's no time to mope! *(CAMBRIDGE runs on stage and dies on top of SCROOP)* The signs of war advance. No king of England, if not King of France! NOW CLEAN UP THIS MESS!

(ALL exit)

Sneak peek of
King Lear for Kids
ACT 1 SCENE 1
KING LEAR's palace

(enter FOOL entertaining the audience with jokes, dancing, juggling, Hula Hooping... whatever the actor's skill may be; enter KENT)

KENT: Hey, Fool!

FOOL: What did you call me?!

KENT: I called you Fool.

FOOL: That's my name, don't wear it out! *(to audience)* Seriously, that's my name in the play!

(enter LEAR, CORNWALL, ALBANY, GONERIL, REGAN, and CORDELIA)

LEAR: The lords of France and Burgundy are outside. They both want to marry you, Cordelia.

ALL: Ooooooo!

LEAR: *(to audience)* Between you and me she IS my favorite child! *(to the girls)* Daughters, I need to talk to you about something. It's a really big deal.

GONERIL & REGAN: Did you buy us presents?

LEAR: This is even better than presents!

GONERIL & REGAN: Goody, goody!!!

CORDELIA: Father, your love is enough for me.

LEAR: Give me the map there, Kent. Girls, I'm tired. I've made a decision: Know that we - and by 'we' I mean 'me' - have divided in three our kingdom...

KENT: Whoa! Sir, dividing the kingdom may cause chaos! People could die!

FOOL: Well, this IS a tragedy...

LEAR: You worry too much, Kent. I'm giving it to my daughters so their husbands can be rich and powerful... like me!

CORNWALL & ALBANY: Sweet!

GONERIL & REGAN: Wait... what?

CORDELIA: This is olden times. That means that everything we own belongs to our husbands.

GONERIL & REGAN: Olden times stink!

CORDELIA: Truth.

LEAR: So, my daughters, tell your daddy how much you love him. Goneril, our eldest-born, speak first.

GONERIL: Sir, I love you more than words can say! More than outer space, puppies and cotton candy! I love you more than any child has ever loved a father in the history of the entire world, dearest Pops!

CORDELIA: *(to audience)* Holy moly! Surely, he won't be fooled by that. *(to self)* Love, and be silent.

LEAR: Thanks, sweetie! I'm giving you this big chunk of the kingdom here. What says our second daughter, Our dearest Regan, wife to Cornwall? Speak.

REGAN: What she said, Daddy... times a thousand!

CORDELIA: *(to audience)* What?! I love my father more than either of them. But I can't express it in words. My love's more richer than my tongue.

LEAR: Wow, Regan! You get this big hunk of the kingdom. Cordelia, what can you tell me to get this giant piece of kingdom as your own? Speak.

CORDELIA: Nothing, my lord.

LEAR: Nothing?!?

CORDELIA: Nothing.

LEAR: Come on, now. Nothing will come of nothing.

CORDELIA: I love you as a daughter loves her father.

LEAR: Try a little, harder, sweetie!

CORDELIA: Why are my sisters married if they give you all their love?

LEAR: How did you get so mean?

CORDELIA: Father, I will not insult you by telling you my love is like... as big as a whale.

LEAR: *(getting mad)* Fine. I'll split your share between your sisters.

REGAN, GONERIL, & CORNWALL: Yessss!

KENT: Whoa! Let's all just calm down a minute!

LEAR: Peace, Kent! You don't want to mess with me right now. I told you she was my favorite...

GONERIL & REGAN: What!?

LEAR: ...and she can't even tell me she loves me more than a whale? Nope. Now I'm mad.

KENT: Royal Lear, really...

LEAR: Kent, I'm pretty emotional right now! You better not try to talk me out of this...

KENT: Sir, you're acting ... insane.

Sneak peek of
Two Gentlemen of Verona for Kids

ANTONIO: It's not nothing.

PROTEUS: Ahhhhh......It's a letter from Valentine, telling me what a great time he's having in Milan, yeah... that's what it says!

ANTONIO: Awesome! Glad to hear it! Because, you leave tomorrow to join Valentine in Milan.

PROTEUS: What!? Dad! No way! I don't want... I mean, I need some time. I've got some things to do.

ANTONIO: Like what?

PROTEUS: You know...things! Important things! And stuff! Lots of stuff!

ANTONIO: No more excuses! Go pack your bag. *(ANTONIO begins to exit)*

PROTEUS: Fie!

ANTONIO: What was that?

PROTEUS: Fiiii......ne with me, Pops! *(ANTONIO exits)* I was afraid to show my father Julia's letter, lest he should take exceptions to my love; and my own lie of an excuse made it easier for him to send me away.

ANTONIO: *(Offstage)* Proteus! Get a move on!!

PROTEUS: Fie!!!

(exit)

ACT 2 SCENE 1

(enter VALENTINE and SPEED following)

VALENTINE: Ah, Silvia, Silvia! *(heavy sighs)*

SPEED: *(mocking)* Madam Silvia! Madam Silvia! Gag me.

VALENTINE: Knock it off! You don't know her.

SPEED: Do too. She's the one that you can't stop staring at. Makes me wanna barf.

VALENTINE: I do not stare!

SPEED: You do. AND you keep singing that silly love song. *(sing INSERT SAPPY LOVE SONG)* You used to be so much fun.

VALENTINE: Huh? *(heavy sigh, starts humming SAME LOVE SONG)*

SPEED: Never mind.

VALENTINE: I have loved her ever since I saw her. Here she comes!

SPEED: Great. *(to audience)* Watch him turn into a fool.

(enter SILVIA)

VALENTINE: Hey, Silvia.

SILVIA: Hey, Valentine. What's goin' on?

VALENTINE: Nothin'. What's goin' on with you?

SILVIA: Nothin'.

(pause)

VALENTINE: What are you doing later?

SILVIA: Not sure. Prob-ly nothin'. You?

VALENTINE: Me neither. Nothin'.

SILVIA: Yea?

VALENTINE: Probably.

SPEED: *(to audience)* Kill me now.

SILVIA: Well, I guess I better go.

VALENTINE: Oh, okay! See ya'..

(pause)

SILVIA: See ya' later maybe?

VALENTINE: Oh, yea! Maybe! Yea! Okay!

SILVIA: Bye.

VALENTINE: Bye!

(exit SILVIA)

SPEED: *(aside)* Wow. *(to VALENTINE)* Dude, what the heck was that?

VALENTINE: I think she has a boyfriend. I can tell.

SPEED: Dude! She is so into you! How could you not see that?

VALENTINE: Do you think?

SPEED: Come on. We'll talk it through over dinner. *(to audience)* Fool. Am I right?

(exit)

Sneak peek of
Christmas Carol for Kids

(enter GHOST PRESENT wearing a robe and holding a turkey leg and a goblet)

GHOST PRESENT: Wake up, Scrooge! I am the Ghost of Christmas Present. Look upon me!

SCROOGE: I'm looking. Not that impressed. But let's get on with it.

GHOST PRESENT: Touch my robe! *(SCROOGE touches GHOST PRESENT's robe. Pause. They look at each other)* Er…it must be broken. Guess we walk. Come on. *(they begin walking downstage)*

SCROOGE: Where are we going?

GHOST PRESENT: Your employee, Bob Cratchit's house. Oh look, here we are.

(enter BOB, MRS. CRATCHIT, MARTHA CRATCHIT, and TINY TIM, who has a crutch in one hand; they are all holding bowls)

BOB: *(to audience)* Hi, we're the Cratchit family. We are a REALLY happy family!

MRS. CRATCHIT: *(to audience)* Yes, but we're REALLY poor, too. Thanks to HIS boss! *(pointing at BOB)*

MARTHA: *(to audience)* Yeah, as you can see our bowls are empty. *(shows empty bowl)* We practically survive off air.

TINY TIM: *(to audience)* But we're happy!

MRS. CRATCHIT: *(to audience; overly sappy)* Because we have each other.

TINY TIM: And love!

SCROOGE: *(to GHOST PRESENT)* Seriously, are they for real?

GHOST PRESENT: Yep! Adorable, isn't it?

BOB: A merry Christmas to us all.

TINY TIM: God bless us every one!

SCROOGE: Spirit, tell me if Tiny Tim will live.

GHOST PRESENT: *(puts hands to head as if looking into the future)* Ooooo, not so good...I see a vacant seat in the poor chimney corner, and a crutch without an owner. If SOMEBODY doesn't change SOMETHING, the child will die.

SCROOGE: No, no! Say he will be spared.

GHOST PRESENT: Nope, can't do that, sorry. Unless SOMEONE decides to change... hint, hint.

BOB: A Christmas toast to my boss, Mr. Scrooge! The founder of the feast!

MRS. CRATCHIT: *(angrily)* Oh sure, Mr. Scrooge! If he were here I'd give him a piece of my mind to feast upon. What an odious, stingy, hard, unfeeling man!

BOB: Dear, it's Christmas day. He's not THAT bad. *(Pause)* He's just... THAT sad. *(BOB holds up his bowl)* Come on, kids, to Scrooge! He probably needs it more than us!

MARTHA & TINY TIM: *(holding up their bowls)* To Scrooge!

MRS. CRATCHIT: *(muttering)* Thanks for nothing.

BOB: That's not nice.

MARTHA: And we Cratchits are ALWAYS nice. Read the book, Mom.

MRS. CRATCHIT: Sorry.

(the CRATCHIT FAMILY exits)

SCROOGE: She called me odious! Do I really smell that bad?

GHOST PRESENT: Odious doesn't mean you stink. Although in this case you do... According to the dictionary, odious means "unequivocally detestable." I mean, you are a toad sometimes Mr. Scrooge.

SCROOGE: Wow... that's kind of... mean.

Sneak peek of
The Tempest for Kids

PROSPERO: Hast thou, spirit, performed to point the tempest that I bade thee?

ARIEL: What? Was that English?

PROSPERO: *(Frustrated)* Did you make the storm hit the ship?

ARIEL: Why didn't you say that in the first place? Oh yeah! I rocked that ship! They didn't know what hit them.

PROSPERO: Why, that's my spirit! But are they, Ariel, safe?

ARIEL: Not a hair perished.

PROSPERO: Woo-hoo! All right. We've got more work to do.

ARIEL: Wait a minute. You're still going to free me, right, Master?

PROSPERO: Oh, I see. Is it sooooo terrible working for me? Huh? Remember when I saved you from that witch? Do you? Remember when that blue-eyed hag locked you up and left you for dead? Who saved you? Me, that's who!

ARIEL: I thank thee, master.

PROSPERO: I will free you in two days, okay? Sheesh. Patience is a virtue, or haven't you heard. Right. Where was I? Oh yeah... I need you to disguise yourself like a sea nymph and then... *(PROSPERO whispers something in ARIEL'S ear)* Got it?

ARIEL: Got it. *(ARIEL exits)*

PROSPERO: *(to MIRANDA)* Awake, dear heart, awake!

(MIRANDA yawns loudly)

PROSPERO: Shake it off. Come on. We'll visit Caliban, my slave.

MIRANDA: The witch's son? You mean the MONSTER! He's creepy and stinky!!!

PROSPERO: Mysterious and sneaky,

MIRANDA: Altogether freaky,

MIRANDA & PROSPERO: He's Caliban the slave!!! *(snap, snap!)*

PROSPERO: *(Calls offstage)* What, ho! Slave! Caliban!

(enter CALIBAN)

CALIBAN: Oh, look it's the island stealers! This is my home! My mother, the witch, left it to me and now you treat me like dirt.

MIRANDA: Oh boo-hoo! I used to feel sorry for you, I even taught you our language, but you tried to hurt me so now we have to lock you in that cave.

CALIBAN: I wish I had never learned your language!

PROSPERO: Go get us wood! If you don't, I'll rack thee with old cramps, and fill all thy bones with aches!

CALIBAN: *(to AUDIENCE)* He's so mean to me! But I have to do what he says. ANNOYING! *(exit CALIBAN)*

(enter FERDINAND led by "invisible" ARIEL)

ARIEL: *(Singing)* Who let the dogs out?! Woof, woof, woof!! *(Spookily)* The watchdogs bark; bow-wow, bow-wow!

FERDINAND: *(Dancing across stage)* Where should this music be? Where is it taking me! What's going on?

Sneak peek of
Hamlet for Kids

(enter GERTRUDE and POLONIUS)

GERTRUDE: What's up, Polonius?

POLONIUS: I am going to hide and spy on your conversation with Hamlet!

GERTRUDE: Oh, okay.

(POLONIUS hides somewhere, enter HAMLET very mad, swinging his sword around)

HAMLET: MOM!!! I AM VERY MAD!

GERTRUDE: Ahhh! You scared me!

(POLONIUS sneezes from hiding spot)

HAMLET: *(not seeing POLONIUS)* How now, a rat? Who's hiding? *(stabs POLONIUS)*

POLONIUS: O, I am slain! Ohhhh the pain! *(dies on stage)*

GERTRUDE: Oh me, what has thou done?

HAMLET: Oops, I thought that was Claudius. Hmph, oh well... as I was saying, I AM MAD you married uncle Claudius!

GERTRUDE: Oh that, yeah, sorry. *(in a motherly voice)* Now, you just killed Polonius, clean up this mess and go to your room!

HAMLET: Okay Mom.

(ALL exit)

ACT 4 SCENES 1-3

(enter GERTRUDE and CLAUDIUS)

GERTRUDE: Ahhh, Dear?

CLAUDIUS: Yeah?

GERTRUDE: Ummmm, you would not believe what I have seen tonight! Polonius is dead.

CLAUDIUS: WHAT!?

GERTRUDE: Yeah, Hamlet was acting a little crazy, Polonius sneezed or something, then Hamlet yelled, "A rat, a rat!" and then WHACK! It was over.

CLAUDIUS: *(very angry)* HAMLET!!!! GET OVER HERE NOW!!!!!

(enter HAMLET)

CLAUDIUS: *(very casual)* Hey, what's up?

HAMLET: What noise, who calls on Hamlet? What do you want?

CLAUDIUS: Now, Hamlet. Where's Polonius' body?

HAMLET: I'm not telling!

CLAUDIUS: Oh come on, please tell me!!! Please! With a cherry on top! Where is Polonius?

HAMLET: Oh, all right. He's over there, up the stairs into the lobby. *(points offstage)*

(POLONIUS enters and dies again)

CLAUDIUS: Ewe... he's a mess! Hamlet, I am sending you off to England.

HAMLET: Fine! Farewell, dear Mother. And I'm taking this with me! *(HAMLET grabs POLONIUS and takes him offstage)*

(all exit but CLAUDIUS)

CLAUDIUS: *(to audience)* I have arranged his execution in England! *(laughs evilly as he exits)* Muwahahaha...

ABOUT THE AUTHOR

BRENDAN P. KELSO, came to writing modified Shakespeare scripts when he was taking time off from work to be at home with his newly born son. "It just grew from there". Within months, he was being asked to offer classes in various locations and acting organizations along the Central Coast of California. Originally employed as an engineer, Brendan never thought about writing. However, his unique personality, humor, and love for engaging the kids with The Bard has led him to leave the engineering world and pursue writing as a new adventure in life! He has always believed, "the best way to learn is to have fun!" Brendan makes his home on the Central Coast of California and loves to spend time with his wife and son.

CAST AUTOGRAPHS

Made in the USA
Monee, IL
26 September 2021